# The Adam Joshua Capers

The Monster in the Third Dresser Drawer
The Kid Next Door
Superkid!
The Show-and-Tell War

## And Coming Soon

The Halloween Monster
George Takes a Bow-Wow!
Turkey Trouble
The Christmas Ghost
Nelson in Love
Serious Science
The Baby Blues

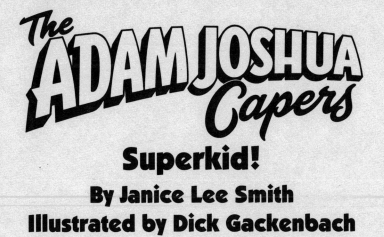

# The ADAM JOSHUA Capers

## Superkid!

By Janice Lee Smith

Illustrated by Dick Gackenbach

HarperTrophy®
*A Division of* HarperCollins*Publishers*

Harper Trophy® is a registered trademark
of HarperCollins Publishers Inc.

*Previously published as part of* The Kid Next Door and Other Headaches:
*Stories About Adam Joshua*

Trophy ISBN 0-06-442005-1
First Harper Trophy edition, 1995.

# Contents

# Superkid!

# Superkid!

"The new Superman movie is coming!" the man on TV told Adam Joshua. "You've got to see it!"

"The new Superman movie is coming!" Adam Joshua yelled, zooming out to the tree house to tell his friend Nelson. "We've got to see it!"

"Well, that will be nice, Adam Joshua," said Nelson, as he swept his side of the tree house. "I like movies."

"Nice?" said Adam Joshua. "Like? Nelson, it's not just a movie. It's the real life story of Superman. We love Superman. He's our hero. We've been waiting for this movie for a long time."

"You've been waiting, maybe. But I

think I've outgrown superheroes," Nelson said. "I just don't believe in Superman anymore. He's a legend."

Adam Joshua could hardly believe Nelson had said that.

"You believe in other people who are legends, Nelson," he said. "You believe in Santa Claus."

Nelson stopped sweeping for a minute to think about it.

"Santa Claus brings me presents and candy," he said, getting back to work. "That makes a difference, you know, Adam Joshua."

———

Adam Joshua practiced each day to get ready for Superman. He practiced speeding faster than a bullet, and he practiced being more powerful than a locomotive, and he practiced bending bars of steel in his bare hands.

"Put that fork down," his mother said,

catching him at it. "That's the third one this week."

"I'm just visiting," Adam Joshua told her. "From a distant planet. If I were you," he said, "I'd be nicer about forks."

His mother looked him straight in the eye and bent the fork back to its shape in her bare hands.

"Then again," Adam Joshua said, watching her, "it's entirely up to you how

to treat your guests."

———

"Almost," the man on TV told Adam Joshua.

"Almost," Adam Joshua called out his bedroom window to Nelson.

"Fine, Adam Joshua," Nelson called back from his bedroom window next door.

Adam Joshua practiced looking through doors with his X-ray vision. He practiced his leaping and bounding and flying.

He practiced fast changes.

"Out," said his mother. "Out of the pantry, and out of the kitchen, and into the backyard while you're at it."

"But it's all I've got," said Adam Joshua, coming out of the kitchen pantry with one pant leg on, and one shoe on, and no shirt on, and the Superman cape his mother made him twisted around his neck.

"I don't have a phone booth," he told her. "But this is near the phone, so I use it."

6

"No, you don't," said his mother, shoving him right out the back door, and tossing his clothes after him.

"Don't forget I'm just visiting," Adam Joshua shouted as the back door slammed. "From another planet!" he yelled.

"And she's going to feel really terrible when she finds out she's treated a guest that way," he muttered to his shoe as he finished getting dressed.

———

"Out!" shouted Nelson. "Out of the tree house, Adam Joshua! All of your jumping around and shouting at things is driving me crazy and scaring my fish."

"But Nelson," said Adam Joshua, rescuing, their turtle, Clyde/Irving, from his box and whizzing him right by Nelson's head. "You're my best friend, Nelson," said Adam Joshua. "You should understand."

"I don't understand anything," said Nelson, rescuing Clyde/Irving from Adam

Joshua and putting him back in his box. "I don't understand you," said Nelson, untying the Superman cape from under Adam Joshua's chin. "Grown kids don't fly around wearing capes, Adam Joshua!" yelled Nelson, flinging the cape down the tree house stairs. "Out!" he shouted.

Adam Joshua knocked on Clyde/Irving's shell before he went.

"I'm here if you need me," said Adam Joshua. "Just whistle and I'll come."

———

"You only need to wait a little longer," said the man on TV.

"Great Galaxies!" said Adam Joshua.

"I may look meek and mild-mannered to you," he told Amanda Jane, flying by his baby sister on his way to supper and stopping to give her a kiss, "but underneath it all," he said, "I'm a kid of iron."

"Kryptonite!" he shouted when he saw the bowl of broccoli on the table.

"Take it away, take it away!" he yelled, throwing up an arm to shield himself from the sight, and falling off his chair, and rolling around on the floor getting ready to die.

"It'll do me in," he whispered.

Amanda Jane leaned out of her high chair to see what was doing him in and dropped a carrot in his ear.

"If the kryptonite doesn't do you in, I'm going to," his mother said, putting extra broccoli on his plate.

———

Nelson was playing in his yard after supper with Henry, his little brother. Nelson put his arms around Henry to protect him the minute Adam Joshua showed up.

"Don't you dare try to fly with this baby," said Nelson.

"Nelson," said Adam Joshua, "if it wasn't for Superman the world would be terrible.

"Superman," said Adam Joshua, "saves people, and stops trains when they're running away, and holds up bridges when they're cracking.

"Superman," said Adam Joshua, "catches bad guys, and helps good guys, and never tells a lie."

"Superman," said Nelson, picking up Henry to go inside, "is made up and I've outgrown him."

"Superman really likes kids," said Adam Joshua. "And he'd be really mad if he knew you felt that way!"

———

"It's here! It's here!" the man on TV shouted at Adam Joshua.

"And about time!" Adam Joshua shouted right along.

He flew down the hall, and through the living room, and into the kitchen, and he picked up Amanda Jane on his way by.

11

"Baby's getting heavy," he panted, sort-of-flying into the living room again, and putting Amanda Jane down with a *splot* on the floor, and sitting himself down with one too.

"Put that baby down," his mother said, after he already had. "You can't do that!" she said.

"Used to be able to," Adam Joshua said, panting hard.

———

Adam Joshua found his Superman undershorts in a corner of the closet. He found his Superman undershirt stuffed down in the bottom of his hamper.

"Still looks fine," he said, pounding the wrinkles out of them with his fist.

He looked through his shirts until he found an old one with only one button left. He could unbutton it in a hurry in case he was needed.

Adam Joshua pulled his Superman cape out of his closet, and his Superman blue pants out from under his bed, and his Superman glasses out from the drawer where he kept things like that.

"I can't believe it," said Adam Joshua, looking at a new hole George, his dog, had chewed in his cape.

He put on his one-button shirt, and the cape with the hole in it, and he put on his blue pants, and he put on his glasses.

George walked by the door, and backed up to come in, and looked at Adam Joshua dressed like Superman, and growled.

Adam Joshua got down, nose to nose

with George, and growled back.

———

"Fifteen minutes," his father called. "The baby-sitter for Amanda Jane's already here."

"Just finishing up," Adam Joshua called back. He found his Superman ring and his Superman medal and put them on. He dug for his Superman cologne, and he splashed some behind his ears. He slipped on his red galoshes.

Then he looked in the mirror.

Superman looked right back at him.

"Don't you worry," Adam Joshua said. "Your identity's safe with me."

"I can't believe it," said Nelson, standing in the doorway, looking at Adam Joshua dressed up in his cape, and the galoshes, and the glasses.

"I can't believe it, either," said Adam Joshua, looking at Nelson dressed in his best shirt, and his best shoes, and his tie.

"I like ties," said Nelson.

———

When they got to the movie theater there was a big line waiting.

"Waiting again," Adam Joshua sighed, as they took their place at the end of the line.

In the line there were kids talking about Superman, and acting like Superman, and in line there were some kids who dressed up to look like him too.

"I just don't believe it," Nelson kept saying, and he kept right on straightening his tie each time he said it.

Adam Joshua turned around and looked eye-to-eye into the eyes of other glasses just like his.

Adam Joshua didn't blink. The other kid didn't blink.

Adam Joshua reached down slowly to the one button on his shirt, and unbuttoned it.

16

"Pow!" he yelled, pulling open his shirt to show his true identity.

The other kid didn't say anything. He reached down and unbuttoned three buttons on his shirt and showed Adam Joshua an undershirt just like his.

"Pow!" he whispered.

"Let's get this line moving," Adam Joshua said, turning around and buttoning his shirt again. "There are some strange characters here," he told his father.

———

Adam Joshua picked the row of seats, and then he picked his seat.

"Perfect," he said.

A tall man with a lot of hair came and sat down right in front of him.

Adam Joshua changed seats with his mother, and he changed seats with his father, and he made Nelson change seats with him.

"Now, that's fine," he said, as he got

everyone settled down again. "Now, every-one sit quiet," said Adam Joshua as the lights went down and the screen lit up with Superman flying fast across it.

Adam Joshua jumped out of his seat to fly right along.

"Shh," said his mother. "Shh," said three people behind him.

"Adam Joshua," said Nelson. "Sit down!"

---

Superman flew high and flew low and caught everybody bad in between.

Superman waged a ceaseless battle against crime. Adam Joshua waged it right up there with him.

Superman fought hard for the truth, and he fought hard for justice, and he fought super hard for The American Way. Adam Joshua was by his side.

Superman kissed his favorite girl.

"That's terrible," said Adam Joshua. scrunching down in his seat with his hands over his eyes.

"You can't trust anybody, Adam Joshua," said Nelson, scrunching down in the seat beside him with his eyes covered too.

———

"The biggest drink," Adam Joshua whispered to his father about refreshments. "The one that comes in the Superman glass you get to keep."

"You can't drink all that," his father whispered back. "That's more than you can handle."

"The biggest," Adam Joshua said, forgetting to whisper. "In the glass."

"Shh," the three people in back and his mother all said.

"I'll just take the little drink," whispered Nelson. "I don't need a glass to keep."

Adam Joshua's drink came in a white shiny glass. Adam Joshua had to hold it with two hands, and he used his knee to hold it up from underneath.

While the villains were looking for Superman, Adam Joshua drank. While Superman was looking for the villains, Adam Joshua drank. While everybody talked about everybody looking for everybody, Adam Joshua drank.

By the time everybody was through talking and Superman and the villains had found each other and were getting ready to fight, Adam Joshua was through drinking and had to go to the bathroom.

"Shh," said his mother as he got up and

made his way across a lot of people's knees to get to the aisle. "Shh, shh, shh," said the three people behind.

By the time Adam Joshua got back the fight was finished.

"You missed the best part," whispered Nelson.

————

"Not bad," Nelson said calmly, straightening his tie and yawning as they walked out of the theater. Adam Joshua glared at Nelson and flashed his shirt open wide.

All the way home, Nelson talked with Adam Joshua's parents about the movie.

"Nice special effects," Nelson told Adam Joshua's father.

"Good photography too," he said.

All the way home, Adam Joshua thought about looking like Superman and flying like Superman, and fighting evil the way Superman fights it.

"Pow!" Adam Joshua whispered to himself.

"I especially enjoyed the plot," said Nelson.

At home, Adam Joshua rescued George, who was sleeping.

George, who was sleeping, woke up and barked, and saw it was Adam Joshua rescuing him, and licked his nose.

"No thanks needed," said Adam Joshua.

Adam Joshua rescued Amanda Jane, who was sleeping.

"Cut that out!" said his mother, putting Amanda Jane back to bed.

Adam Joshua rescued his mother right where she stood, patting Amanda Jane back to sleep again.

"My hero," his mother said, bending down to kiss him.

"Last time *she* gets saved," Adam Joshua said, flying out of the room, spitting a lot.

Out his window, Adam Joshua could see

Nelson untying his tie in the mirror and talking to his fish.

Adam Joshua flew around his room four times with his cape spread wide behind him.

"Adam Joshua, Superkid!" he said, screeching to a stop in front of his mirror.

Looking back at him was Adam Joshua in a cape that had a hole chewed there by George. Looking back at him was Adam Joshua in a shirt with one button, and a wrinkled undershirt, and red galoshes, and blue pants that had grown too little.

"We were great!" said both Adam Joshuas.

———

He took off his cape. He took off his shirt with one button, and his blue pants, and his underwear, and his galoshes. He sort of folded everything and stuffed it all away in his bottom dresser drawer. He put on his pajamas with Superman flying fast across the top.

Adam Joshua turned out the light and crawled into bed with George.

"Don't you worry," he told George. "I remember every minute and everything that Superman did in the movie, and I'll tell you all about it."

George yawned and closed his eyes.

"But you mustn't get too excited about it," said Adam Joshua, "or you'll never get to sleep."

Adam Joshua told George about the flying and the fighting.

He didn't tell him a thing about the kissing.

Out his window, Adam Joshua could see Nelson telling his fish about the photography and the plot.

"I'm really worried about that kid," Adam Joshua told George.

Adam Joshua saw Nelson go into his

closet and pull the door shut.

Adam Joshua waited but Nelson didn't come out.

"Excuse me," Adam Joshua said, scooting out from underneath George, "I'll finish telling you things in a minute."

Adam Joshua stood at his window and used his binoculars to study Nelson's room. Everything in Nelson's room looked very neat. His tie was on the dresser. His fish were asleep in their bowl. Nelson was in his closet.

Adam waited. Nelson didn't come out.

Adam Joshua studied the bottom of the closet door with his binoculars to see if Nelson was trying to send smoke signals or messages out underneath it. But there was no sign from Nelson.

All of a sudden Nelson's closet door flew open and Nelson flew out of it, and he flew around his room twice with his arms out and his cape spread wide behind him.

27

The closet door banged back all the way, and on the inside of it Adam Joshua could see a big picture of Superman.

"Great Galaxies!" said Adam Joshua.

Nelson had on his red rubber boots, and blue pants, and a red and blue striped shirt. He had on a cape that Adam Joshua had never seen before, but it must have been a cape that Nelson had in his closet all along.

"You'll never believe it either," Adam Joshua said, waking up George and carrying him to the window.

Nelson zoomed around his room, and he flew high and flew low, and he picked up his fish to try flying with them.

Adam Joshua and George watched as Nelson stopped to put his fish back on their table and mopped up fish water with his cape. Then Nelson climbed up on his bed to get a leaping start. He looked out the window.

 28

Adam Joshua ducked so Nelson wouldn't see him, and he made George duck too.

When he came up again, Nelson's shade was down.

"I know just how you feel," Adam Joshua said as he took George over and dumped him in bed. He went to his bottom dresser drawer and got out his cape.

"But I don't want to hear a word about it," he said, crawling in bed with George and using the cape to cover them both.

# A Visit from Cynthia

Nelson's cousin, Cynthia, was coming to stay for a bit.

"And it's going to be awful, Adam Joshua," said Nelson. "I haven't seen her since I was a baby, but I know she's a girl. And what are we going to do with a girl?"

There were some kinds of girls Adam Joshua liked, but there were other kinds he couldn't stand. "What kind of a girl, Nelson?" Adam Joshua asked.

"Well, my mother says she's sweet," said Nelson, "but I think she means gooey. And my mother says she's quiet and good," said Nelson, "but I'll bet that means she won't want to do any of the

POW!

things we like to do. I think we're in a lot of trouble, Adam Joshua."

Adam Joshua nodded along with Nelson. That was exactly the kind of girl he hated. He sat for a minute thinking about it.

"You know, Superman seems to like all kinds of girls," he finally said. "And you know, Nelson, I've always worried about that."

———

When Cynthia got there, she was very quiet.

"Just a little shy," said Nelson's mother, straightening a bow on one of Cynthia's braids and giving her a pat on the shoulder to help her feel brave.

"You boys be gentle with her," whispered Nelson's mother. "She's older than you but she's nervous and shy and needs time to adjust. Very gentle," said Nelson's mother, straightening the other one of Cynthia's bows and going inside.

Adam Joshua and Nelson stood staring at Cynthia, and Cynthia stood staring at the ground.

Cynthia didn't say anything.

Nelson didn't say anything.

"Nice bows," said Adam Joshua.

Cynthia stopped staring at the ground and raised her eyes and stood staring at Adam Joshua and Nelson. She put a hand on a bow and smiled.

It was a horrible smile. It was a smile full of big yellow teeth, and full of broken braces that glittered in the sun, and it had a lot of meanness mixed right in.

Cynthia smiled and yanked at her bows, and her hair came out of its braids and shot out in spikes all over her head.

"Move it!" said Cynthia, throwing the bows over her shoulders.

"Follow me!" she said, marching for the tree house. "We've got a lot to get done,

and I've only got a few days to get things organized."

Cynthia pulled a pair of sunglasses out of her pocket and put them on. They were the kind of sunglasses that hid eyes, and had mirrors where the lenses should be.

Adam Joshua hated sunglasses like that.

"I thought your mother said she'd be sweet and quiet," Adam Joshua whispered, following along scared.

"My mother's been wrong before," whispered Nelson, scared and right behind him.

In the tree house Cynthia got things organized. She put Nelson and Adam Joshua in a corner and made them stay there.

"You little kids don't get in my way," she told them. "Don't even think it!"

"This junk's got to go," said Cynthia, picking up their pinecone collections, and

POW! 38

their rock collections, and their marble collections, and their seashells, and dumping them all over the side.

"Kid stuff," said Cynthia, ripping down the Superman poster, and sending it over the side too.

"Now, hold on a minute!" shouted Adam Joshua. He stood up and faced Cynthia at about her neck.

Cynthia looked Adam Joshua over closely.

"At home I've got big snakes," she said. "They eat rats whole. And you're not much bigger than a rat," she said, picking Adam Joshua up and putting him back in the corner again.

"The turtle," said Cynthia, slipping Clyde/Irving in her pocket, "is mine."

———

Cynthia put up posters of the kind of monsters that Adam Joshua and Nelson didn't even like to think about. Next she

39

put out her collections.

"Snakeskins," she said, putting out boxes. "Spiders," she said, putting out jars. "And bones, Adam Joshua," she said, waving one under his nose. "I don't have any people bones," Cynthia said, separating the big bones from the small. "Not yet. But I'm working on it."

Cynthia finished getting organized by writing big across the tree house wall.

"CYNTHIA'S PLACE!!!" she wrote.

It looked just like Cynthia's place. There was nothing of Adam Joshua or Nelson left there at all.

———

That night Adam Joshua sat around trying to think what to do about Cynthia.

"I can't think of a thing," he told George.

Later that night, Nelson showed up at Adam Joshua's door with his fishbowl held tight in his arms.

 40

"Adam Joshua," whispered Nelson, "hide my fish. You never can tell what she's going to organize next."

In the morning when Adam Joshua looked out his window, Cynthia was already in the tree house with Nelson tucked in the corner. Cynthia was talking to her spiders. Nelson wasn't saying a word.

"Keep the dog and the baby inside," Adam Joshua told his mother on his way through the kitchen. "Outside they wouldn't stand a chance."

"You don't have to keep coming back," Nelson whispered to Adam Joshua when he climbed into the tree house. "She's not your cousin, and she's not your problem, and you don't have to come."

"I'll come," whispered Adam Joshua. "You're my friend and you need me. Without me," whispered Adam Joshua, looking at Cynthia with her braces glittering in the sun, "she'd have you eaten in no time."

"Sit down and get quiet," said Cynthia.

Adam Joshua and Nelson sat down. They got quiet.

"It's my tree house now, and we go by my rules now, and now you do what I say," said Cynthia, standing there with her hands on her hips, looking down at Adam Joshua and Nelson.

"Any questions?" asked Cynthia.

Nobody had any questions.

In Cynthia's sunglasses Adam Joshua

 42

could see himself and Nelson sitting quiet and little and hardly there at all. While Cynthia talked the sun made her braces flash like barbed wire. When Cynthia stopped talking and smiled, it was even worse.

"Superman," Adam Joshua whispered to Nelson, "would know what to do about this.

"Superman," Adam Joshua whispered to Nelson, "would take care of her in no time."

"Terrific, Adam Joshua," Nelson whispered back, trying to get more comfortable in the corner. "Then get him fast," he said.

"Today we play games," said Cynthia. "I love games."

Cynthia knew games that made Adam Joshua and Nelson shiver in their shoes.

"In this game," Cynthia said, "I pretend to roast you alive and eat you whole."

"In the next game," Cynthia said, "I pretend to skin you first."

Adam Joshua and Nelson played

Cynthia's games, and they played by her rules, and they did what she told them to do.

They hated it.

They kept playing games, and then Cynthia got hungry and made Adam Joshua and Nelson get her food. They hated that too, but they did it.

Cynthia ate and then she got sleepy. She made Adam Joshua and Nelson polish the bones in her collection while she took a nap in the tree house.

"And I only sleep with one eye," said Cynthia. "The other one will be wide awake watching you."

———

"I should do something, Adam Joshua," said Nelson, polishing hard on a bone. "She's my cousin and it's up to me. It's just," he said, "that I don't know what to do. I'm not very brave, Adam Joshua," said Nelson.

 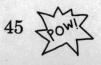

Adam Joshua felt the same way about Nelson, but he didn't think he should let Nelson know.

"You've helped me with a lot of my problems, Nelson," he said, polishing hard too. "Why, you've been brave about all my problems."

"Problems that belong to other people are easy, Adam Joshua," said Nelson. "Cousins that belong to you," he said, picking up a new bone and sighing, "really aren't the same thing at all."

That night, Adam Joshua lay on his bed and worried some more about Nelson. George lay beside him worrying too.

"Somebody needs to take care of him," Adam Joshua told George.

George growled.

"Right," said Adam Joshua, rubbing George's nose.

Then he saw Nelson's shade go down and Nelson's hand go up behind it.

"ADAM JOSHUA," the hand wrote, "I HAVE A GREAT IDEA ABOUT—"

Another hand, one wearing a spider ring, came up under the shade and grabbed the hand belonging to Nelson. The hand took away the marker and rolled the shade up with a snap.

Adam Joshua put on his Superman cape and flew around the room with George right behind.

"Zam, zap, Cynthia!" he shouted. "Zow, zing!

47

"POW!" he yelled out his window over at Nelson's window and Cynthia. Then he pulled his shade down fast just in case Cynthia was looking out and could see him.

———

"What do you do about a bully?" Adam Joshua asked his mother the next morning at breakfast. "A big one. And mean."

"Most bullies are really cowards," said his mother. "Most bullies are afraid of things, and they don't feel very good about themselves, so they act like bullies. Usually a bully will back off if you stand up to him."

"Her," said Adam Joshua.

"Her," said his mother.

"What if your bully isn't usual?" asked Adam Joshua. "What if you stand up to her and she gets mad?"

"Then you get hurt," said his mother.

"That's pretty much what I thought," said Adam Joshua, pushing the rest of his breakfast away.

 48

"You look terrible, Nelson," Adam Joshua whispered to Nelson in the tree house corner. "Why, Nelson, you look really bad."

"Cynthia," said Nelson, "isn't an easy person to live with, Adam Joshua. She plays tricks. The first night she put her biggest hairy spider in my bed, and it crawled right up my pajama leg before I knew it was there. Last night it was a bone under my pillow, and later she threw a snakeskin on me. A person," said Nelson, "doesn't sleep well after that."

"What about your great idea, Nelson?" Adam Joshua asked. "The one you wrote on your shade. What about that?"

"Never mind, Adam Joshua," whispered Nelson, yawning. "It wasn't that great. It wasn't even good."

———

"Today," said Cynthia, "I have a whole list of new games. I'm just going to love

49 POW!

today," she said, and she smiled.

Adam Joshua and Nelson played the new games. They were the worst games they had ever played in their lives. They polished Cynthia's bones, and helped her look in the yard and in the garbage for new ones.

They brought her food.

"Red meat," said Cynthia. "Hard bread. Lemonade."

"She's good around my mother, Adam Joshua," said Nelson, polishing bones while Cynthia slept with one eye. "Around my mother she's fine.

"And even when I tell my mother, Adam Joshua," said Nelson, "even when I tell my mother all about her, my mother doesn't believe it all. My mother says that nobody that good can be that bad.

"Then," said Nelson, rubbing his polishing arm for a minute, "my mother says even if she was that bad, we'd still have to

put up with most of it. My mother says when you have guests sometimes you have to put up with a lot. Cynthia's more than a lot to put up with, Adam Joshua," said Nelson. "She's a whole lot more."

"We could always say no, Nelson," whispered Adam Joshua, polishing his bone even harder as Cynthia woke up and started stretching. "I'll bet we could just say no," Adam Joshua whispered again, trying to make his whisper sound brave.

"Once," said Cynthia, standing up to finish her stretch, "there was a kid I told to do something and he told me he didn't want to do it. He said, 'No.'"

Adam Joshua got up fast to go get Cynthia some more lemonade.

"He's still looking for his teeth," Cynthia yelled after him.

———

"What do you do when you think you should be brave, but you don't know how

51 POW!

to be?" Adam Joshua asked his father. "What do you do if you're afraid to be brave?"

"Everyone's afraid to be brave," Adam Joshua's father told him. "Otherwise they wouldn't need to be brave to do what they do.

"But you have to be wise about being brave," said Adam Joshua's father, scratching George behind the ears until he was almost asleep. "You have to decide if it's worth it. Because it's one thing to be brave," said his father, covering Adam Joshua and George up with the blanket, "and it's another thing to be foolish."

---

"I know how you feel," Adam Joshua told George the next morning, when George stood at the door, whining to go out to play.

"I know you want to be with me, and I know you're brave," he told George. "But you need to get smart too," he said, giving

POW!

George a kiss on the nose and leaving him there.

———

"We could hit her, Adam Joshua," said Nelson, while they looked for flies to feed Cynthia's spiders. "You could hit her."

"I'm just not a hitting kind of person," said Adam Joshua. "I didn't even hit when I was a baby. Amanda Jane doesn't even hit." Adam Joshua thought about it. "She bites a bit, though," he said.

"Maybe we could pounce on her, Adam Joshua," said Nelson, killing a fly and looking sad about it. "If you'd pounce first, I'd be right behind you."

"I'm not any good at pouncing either," Adam Joshua said. He got ready to kill a fly and then let it go because it looked like it had things to do.

"If we do anything about her," said Nelson, closing his eyes tight, and hitting a fly fast, "we're going to get hurt. It

POW! 54

seems to me that it's better to do what she wants and wait till she leaves. I don't know how long she'll be here, Adam Joshua," said Nelson. "The hurting could go on for days."

Adam Joshua and Nelson fed flies to spiders, and they fed food to Cynthia, and they settled down to the bones.

"Okay, Nelson," whispered Adam Joshua. "We've put up with a lot so far. We can keep putting up with it. But Nelson," said Adam Joshua, "everybody's got a limit. We've got to have a limit too. We'll put up with things, but we'll have a limit about how much we'll put up with."

"I still wish I was braver," Nelson whispered.

They watched Cynthia pick up a jar of spiders to talk to them. A big hairy one looked like it was talking back.

"Sometimes, Nelson," said Adam Joshua, "you can confuse being brave with being foolish."

Cynthia wrapped a snakeskin around her neck and stroked it.

"Or really dumb," he said.

———

"So don't worry," Adam Joshua told George, scratching him behind the ears to help him get to sleep that night. "We've got our limit, and we can put up with things until then. But I know if we need you," Adam Joshua told George, "you'll be right there."

The first thing Adam Joshua saw when he woke up in the morning was a stick sticking out of Nelson's window. At the end of the stick was a sock, and a note was pinned to it.

"WAR!!!" yelled the note.

Adam Joshua jumped up and got dressed for war.

He got out his Superman underwear, and his blue pants, and his shirt with one button, and he dug his cape and galoshes out of the closet.

"I need you," he told George.

"Out of our way, Amanda Jane," Adam Joshua said, going past his sister in the kitchen, and picking her up to give her a kiss, and putting her out of the way.

"War," he told her, "is no place for a kid."

———

"My fish, Adam Joshua," said Nelson, meeting him under the tree and looking terrible. "I gave you most of my fish," he said, "but I had two that were sick. I kept them home to take care of them, and I hid them away.

"Adam Joshua," said Nelson, looking worse, "she flushed my fish. She found them, and she said nobody could be expected to live with sick fish.

"Adam Joshua," yelled Nelson, "she flushed my fish!"

"Nelson," hollered Adam Joshua, "do you mean we're going to fight because of two fish? Nelson," he shouted, "you

mean we're going to finally get murdered because of two fish? Nelson," said Adam Joshua, sitting on the ground, tired, "I thought she had done something to *you*."

"Adam Joshua," said Nelson, sitting down too, "my fish *are* me." Tears started to roll down his cheeks.

Adam Joshua couldn't stand it when Nelson cried.

"Well, then, don't you worry," he said,

POW!

hugging Nelson hard and wiping away some of the tears with his cape. "A limit's a limit, and a friend's a friend, and war's war," he said, unbuttoning his shirt.

———

"Cynthia," Adam Joshua yelled when Cynthia got to the tree house. "You've pushed us, you've shoved us, and you've bossed us around. Cynthia," yelled Adam Joshua, "you've thrown out our stuff, and you've taken our turtle, and you've made us play games and do things we hate."

"You've flushed my fish," yelled Nelson.

George growled.

"Cynthia," said Adam Joshua, "I'm not good at hitting, but you take one more step and I'm going to hit you."

"And I'm going to help him," said Nelson, standing tall beside Adam Joshua. "And I kick too, Cynthia," said Nelson, quietly. "Hard."

"And I'm going to knock out your teeth," said Cynthia.

————

In the tree house there were pinecone collections, and marble collections, and seashells, and rocks.

Spiders and bones and snakeskins were gone.

The Superman poster was back up, looking a little worse for the wear. Adam Joshua and Nelson looked the same way.

Adam Joshua had a rip in his cape, and a bruise on his shoulder, and a bash on his knuckles, and a black eye.

Nelson had rips in his pants, and a scratch on his cheek, and a foot that felt broken, and an eye like Adam Joshua's.

But they both kept all their teeth.

"And it was worth it, Adam Joshua," said Nelson, stretching out on the floor of the tree house and taking off his shoe to rub his foot.

61

"Well, it was worth it," said Adam Joshua, stretching out too. He got back up.

He took out a marker and drew an X through where it said, " CYNTHIA'S PLACE!!! "

"Not anymore," he said. "THiS PLACE BELONGS TO ADAM JOSHUA AND NELSON," he wrote. " AND ALWAYS WiLL!! "

"Make that Nelson and Adam Joshua," said Nelson.

Adam Joshua knocked on Clyde/Irving's shell.

"You can come out now," he said, "she's gone.

"I'll take George inside, Nelson," said Adam Joshua, going over to where George was resting from fighting Cynthia. One ear had a bend in it, and his tail dragged low.

"Don't even bother getting up," he told George. "I'll carry you all the way.

"After I take George inside, Nelson," said Adam Joshua, "I'll bring your fish out. You can sit with your fish in the tree house, and you'll feel fine."

"No hurry, Adam Joshua," said Nelson. "I'll be glad to see my fish, but I'm feeling fine already. In fact, Adam Joshua," Nelson called after him, "I feel the finest I've felt in all my life!"

Cynthia's sunglasses were lying at the bottom of the tree house ladder.

Adam Joshua picked them up and put them on George so the sun wouldn't get in his eyes.

"Pow!" he said.

**Don't miss:**

# The Show-and-Tell War

● Superman has an archenemy named Lex Luthor. Adam Joshua has an archenemy named Elliot Banks. This year, Adam Joshua's worst fear has come true. Elliot Banks is in his class!

● Adam Joshua's only been in school a few weeks. But he's certain that his dog and his baby sister are lonely at home without him . . . or maybe they're having so much fun that they don't even miss him!

● Show-and-tell used to be fun. But now it's a showdown! Elliot Banks only brings in really expensive stuff. How will Adam Joshua ever compete?